Explore the World of
Exotic Rainforests

Text by Anita Ganeri
Illustrated by Robert Morton

A GOLDEN BOOK • NEW YORK

Western Publishing Company, Inc., Racine, Wisconsin 53404

Contents

Where do rainforests grow?
The major tropical rainforests grow in the hot, equatorial regions of the world, primarily in South America and Africa, Southeast Asia, and in Australasia. Although these rainforests cover only 7 percent of the Earth's land surface, they provide a home for at least half of all the species of animals and plants in the world. They are also the home of many different tribes of people.

What is a rainforest?

A rainforest, or jungle, is a dense tangle of trees, vines, and other plants. Rainforests grow in three layers determined by the different heights of the trees. The tallest trees, growing as tall as 200 feet, are called emergent trees. Below them is a dense green layer of treetops, called the canopy, which grows like a roof over the forest. The canopy may be 20 feet thick. This is where most rainforest animals and birds live. Beneath the canopy is the understory, where smaller trees, such as palms and cycads, grow to about 50 feet tall. The forest floor is a green shadowy place, because very little sunlight can reach it through the thick canopy above. The floor is covered with fallen, rotting leaves, which provide nutrients for young trees and plants.

More about life in the forest

The cassowary, a huge bird that lives in New Guinea and Australia, uses its horny headgear like a battering ram to crash through the forest undergrowth. The cassowary cannot fly, but it is a fast runner.

The rafflesia is the biggest flower in the world. A single flower can be more than 3 feet wide. Rafflesias are also known as carrion flowers, because they smell like rotting meat. This attracts flies, which visit the flowers and pollinate them.

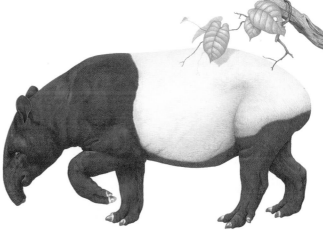

The tapir's striking black-and-white coat helps this animal to hide among the patches of light and shade in the forest. Tapirs have poor eyesight, but they use their trunklike noses to find their way through the forest in search of food.

Where is the biggest rainforest?

The Amazon rainforest in South America is bigger than all the other rainforests in the world put together. The forest grows along the banks of the mighty Amazon River and its tributaries. The river is 3,900 miles long — the world's second-longest river, next to the Nile in Egypt. The Amazon flows from the Andes Mountains in Peru, across South America, and into the Atlantic Ocean off the coast of Brazil. The Amazon River contains two thirds of all the fresh water on Earth.

More about Amazon animals

Caimans are reptiles that are closely related to crocodiles and alligators. They lie in wait for unsuspecting fish, small mammals, and birds, which they snap up with their long, sharp teeth. The largest caimans can grow to more than 7 feet long.

Anacondas are the largest snakes in the world. They can grow to almost 30 feet long and can weigh more than 400 pounds. They are superb swimmers and spend most of their time in the water. They can also climb trees to seek shelter.

Piranhas are small fish that prey on tapirs, cows, and other animals that come to the river to drink. Piranhas attack in schools and can strip a 100-pound animal to the bone in just a few minutes. Their teeth are so sharp that rainforest people make scissors and knives out of them.

What are lianas?

Long, woody, ropelike vines dangle down from the trees in the rainforest canopy. These are called lianas, or bush ropes. These clinging plants are strong enough for a person to climb on, and some are 500 feet long. They do not have their own thick trunks to support them, so they cling to young trees instead. As the trees grow, they take the lianas upward with them. This is how the lianas reach the sunlight, which they need for growth.

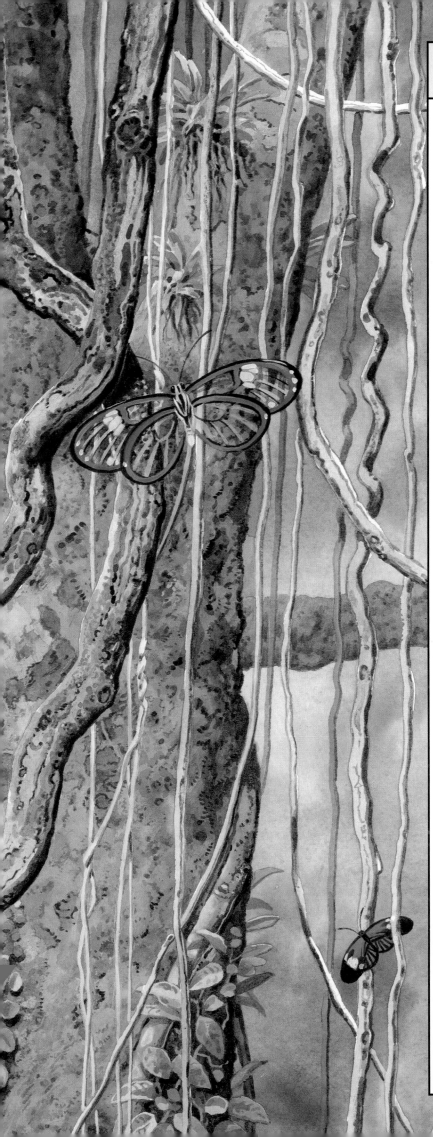

More about climbing plants

Strangler fig seeds sprout high up on another tree's branches. The roots drop down to the ground, where water and nutrients enable the fig to grow into a tree. Over many years, these roots form a thick trellis around the original tree's trunk. Eventually, this tree is smothered and dies and only the strangler fig is left.

Many vines and other clinging plants also use rainforest trees for support. Monkey ladder vines grow in Costa Rica. Some are shaped like spiral staircases, with individual steps. Others have footholds and look like ladders with rungs.

Epiphytes, or air plants, grow on tree branches, with their roots hanging in the air. Since the roots are so far from the soil, epiphytes take in water from the air and get nourishment from leaves and molds growing on the branches.

More about rainforest plants

Why is the rosy periwinkle useful?

The rosy periwinkle from Madagascar contains chemicals that can be used to treat people with leukemia (a cancer of the blood). It has been more successful in curing these people than any of the medicines that were ever used before. The periwinkle is just one of many medicinal plants that are found in the rainforests.

How big is the Amazon water lily?

The giant Amazon water lily has huge leaves, or pads, that grow up to 5 feet across. The leaves float on the surface of the water, supported by thick, air-filled ribs underneath. A lily pad is strong enough for a child to sit on.

How many types of orchid are there?

There are over 30,000 different types of orchid growing all over the world. Many live high up in the rainforest canopy on the branches of trees. A single tree may have as many as 300 orchids growing on it.

What are buttress roots?

Many tall rainforest trees have very shallow roots to hold them up. This is because the nutrients they need are found in the thin top layer of fallen leaves instead of deep in the soil. For extra stability, many trees have huge buttress roots, or supports, growing out of their trunks.

Where do ginger plants grow?
Ginger plants, with their bright red fruit, grow on the shady rainforest floor. The root of the ginger plant is used to season many types of food.

How common is the African violet?
The African violet is very popular and common as a houseplant. But in the wild, the African violet is one of the most threatened plants in the world. They are only found in the African rainforest in Tanzania. They are becoming rarer as the rainforests are being cut down and cleared.

Why do some mushrooms glow in the dark?
At night the rainforest floor may glow with an eerie greenish light. This is made by chemicals inside some species of rainforest mushrooms. No one knows exactly why the mushrooms glow. It may be to protect them from being eaten by beetles.

Why is logging bad for the rainforest?

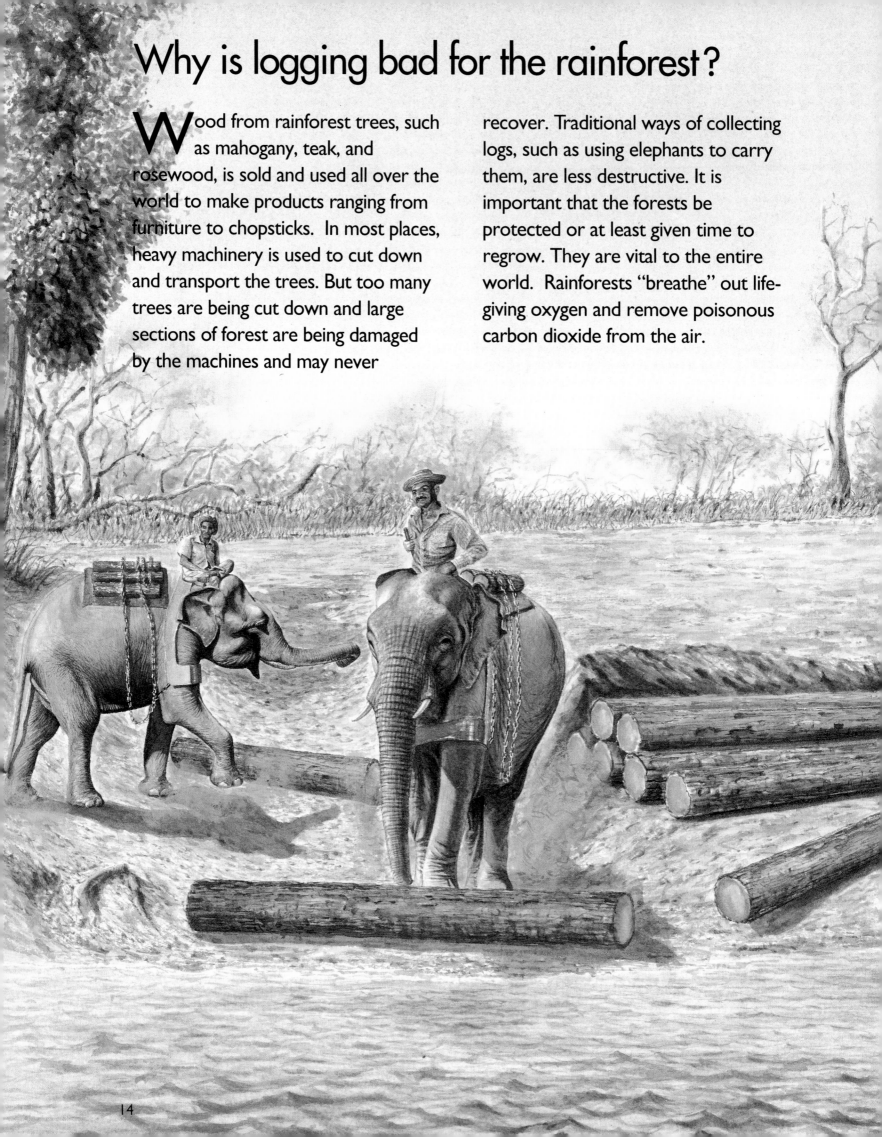

Wood from rainforest trees, such as mahogany, teak, and rosewood, is sold and used all over the world to make products ranging from furniture to chopsticks. In most places, heavy machinery is used to cut down and transport the trees. But too many trees are being cut down and large sections of forest are being damaged by the machines and may never recover. Traditional ways of collecting logs, such as using elephants to carry them, are less destructive. It is important that the forests be protected or at least given time to regrow. They are vital to the entire world. Rainforests "breathe" out life-giving oxygen and remove poisonous carbon dioxide from the air.

How are the rainforests being destroyed?

Logging is not the only way a rainforest is destroyed. When roads are opened by the loggers, people move into new areas of the forest to farm. In addition, many people who once lived outside the forest and have been forced from their homes by land developers have nowhere to live except in the forest. Then even more trees are cut down to open up space for villages and homes. Tribes of rainforest people, who have always lived in harmony with the forest, are being forced out by the newcomers. In the South American rainforest, huge areas have been burned to make way for farms and cattle ranches. As the forest disappears, so do many species of animals and plants. At the present rate of destruction, the rainforests may disappear altogether in 50 years. People and organizations, such as the World Wide Fund for Nature, are now working to save the forest and its inhabitants before it is too late.

More about endangered species

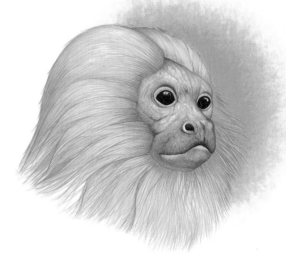

The golden lion tamarin is one of the rarest monkeys in the world. Only about 100 are known to live in the rainforest in Brazil. The tamarin population has suffered as the trees in which the tamarins make their homes have been cut down.

The river terrapin comes from Southeast Asia. There are now very few of these turtles left. The rivers in which they live are being so badly polluted by mining operations, dam building, and destruction of the forest that the terrapins cannot survive.

Okapis, which are related to giraffes, are very timid animals that live only in the rainforests of Zaire, Africa. Okapis were unknown before 1901, and they are already in danger of dying out as their forest home is being destroyed.

How do rainforest people hunt?

The Penan people of Borneo are nomadic hunter-gatherers. Nomads regularly move from place to place when the food supply is used up. They build a new home each time they move. They use the forest's resources to survive, but they are careful not to abuse the forest. For example, they gather fruits and other foods and are skilled hunters, using blowguns with poison darts to kill their prey, primarily monkeys. The Penan people — like other rainforest people who use hunting poisons — know exactly which plants can be used to make the poison. Although the poison kills the animals almost instantly, the meat is safe for people to eat.

More about rainforest people

Why is Chico Mendes famous?

Chico Mendes was the leader of the rubber-tree tapper's union in the state of Acre, Brazil. The union actively campaigned against the destruction of the forest for cattle ranching. In 1988 Chico Mendes was murdered by cattle ranchers. Mendes and the union did succeed in proving that the forest could be used to provide jobs and resources without being destroyed. As a result of these actions, the state of Acre has lost less than 5 percent of the rainforest since Mendes's death.

How do rainforest people live?

The Mbuti tribe of Pygmies, who live in the rainforests of Zaire, Africa, gather nuts and fruits from the forest. They also trap okapi and antelopes in nets and hunt with spears and bows and arrows.

Which people live in longhouses?

The Dayak people of Borneo create a sense of community in their villages by sharing their food, possessions, and work. They live together in enormous wooden houses, called longhouses. These houses are big enough for several families to live in. Some longhouses can accommodate up to 400 people.

Who are medicine men?

Among many rainforest tribes, the medicine men, or shamans (left), are greatly revered for their knowledge and powers. Shamans, who can be men or women, use plants from the forest and ancient mystical rituals to cure sick people. Some of the ancient remedies are being tested by modern pharmaceutical companies for future use.

Are other rainforest people involved in protecting the forests?

The Kayapo Indians of Brazil still practice lip stretching (right) and other tribal traditions. However, they welcome some aspects of modern life, such as canned foods, radios, and clothing. They do not welcome plans to use their forest homes to provide more and more resources for the outside world. For example, they have organized protests and demonstrations against plans to build dams for a hydroelectrical project, which would destroy their villages and flood an area of the forest larger than England and Wales combined.

Where do the Kuna people grow crops?

The Kuna people live on some small islands off the coast of Panama. However, they rely on the mainland rainforest for growing their food. They visit their crops every day, crossing the water in their dugout canoes.

How do Waorani Indians build their homes?

Like the Penan people, the Waorani Indians in Ecuador are a nomadic tribe. Because they are constantly on the move, the Waorani are very skilled at building their own houses. A family can make a temporary shelter out of young trees, vines, and palm leaves in a few hours and build a house in about three days.

Which rainforest bird helps people find honey?

Wild honey is highly prized by West African Pygmies. They have a special way of finding beehives in the treetops. A small bird, called a honeyguide, which loves to eat beeswax, leads them to the nests, flying and calling to show them the way. A Pygmy climbs the tree to the beehive to dig the honey out. He carries a bunch of smoking leaves to sedate the bees so they do not sting him. After he has taken the honey, he leaves the beeswax as a reward for the honeyguide for helping him.

More about rainforest products

Natural rubber comes from rubber trees in the Amazon rainforest. Rubber-tree tappers cut slits in the tree bark and a milky white resin, called latex, oozes out. This is collected in small cups attached to the tree.

Quinine is a drug used to help prevent malaria, a disease that is spread by mosquitoes. It is made from the ground-up bark of the cinchona tree, which is found in the Amazon.

Brazil nuts and cashews, as well as tropical fruits and spices, are examples of rainforest products that can be harvested and sold without damage to the forest. Brazil nuts grow in clusters inside a large fruit. A small rodent, called an agouti, often hoards the nuts and then forgets where it has buried them. The forgotten nuts will grow into new trees.

What are birds of paradise?

Birds of paradise live mainly in the rainforests of Papua New Guinea. Although the female's coloring is quite dull, many males have dazzling, brightly colored feathers and plumes. The males show these off to attract females. One species, Count Raggi's birds of paradise, shown here, fan and shake their feathers to attract as many females as possible. Males often hang upside-down from a branch to display their long red feathers. They grow their brilliant plumage during the mating season. Then they lose their feathers and must grow them again the following year.

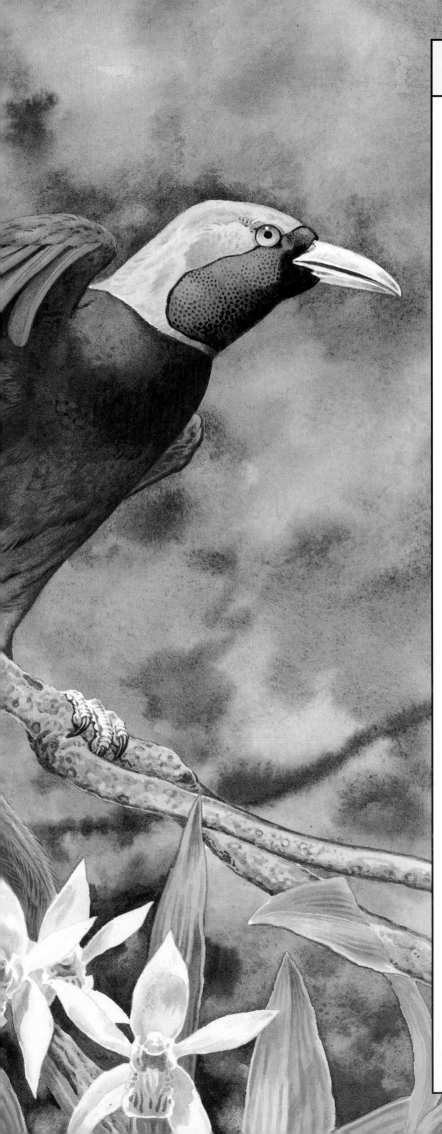

More about bright feathers

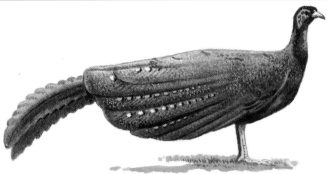

The male great argus pheasant of Southeast Asia has very long tail and wing feathers. The wing feathers are decorated with rows of large "eyes." During its courtship dance, the male fans out its feathers to try to attract a female.

During the mating season, orange-and-black male cock-of-the-rocks gather in a forest clearing to perform their courtship dance. Males try to attract females with their colorful plumage and by their dancing abilities.

Resplendent quetzals are spectacular-looking green-and-crimson birds from Central America. Their tail feathers can be 2 feet long. Aztec chiefs worshipped quetzals as gods and used these feathers in headdresses.

What do hummingbirds eat?

Hummingbirds feed on the sweet nectar deep inside rainforest flowers. Many of these flowers are tube-shaped. The hummingbird uses its long, thin bill to reach inside the flowers and suck out the nectar. A hummingbird visits thousands of flowers a day to get enough food to survive. At each "stop," its feathers get dusted with pollen. The pollen rubs off when the bird visits another flower. In this way, the bird pollinates the flower so it can produce a seed that will grow into a new plant.

Why do toucans have big beaks?

The toco toucan from Brazil has the largest beak of any of the toucans. The male's beak may be more than 8 inches long — about a third of the length of the toucan's body. Despite the beak's great size, it is both light and strong and is used for plucking fruit from branches.

The beak's bright colors may help the toucans to recognize each other. Toucans also use their beaks to toss fruit to each other and to hold pretend beak battles. The colors may also frighten other birds away from their nests so the toucans can steal their eggs and chicks.

More about beaks

Sunbirds from Africa and Asia feed on nectar from tropical flowers. Like hummingbirds, sunbirds have long, thin, curved beaks adapted to reach deep into the flowers. The beaks also have serrated edges for catching insects.

Parrots have sharp, curved beaks that are strong enough to crack open seeds and the hardest nuts, such as Brazil nuts. Parrots also use their beaks for cleaning themselves and to help them climb trees.

Hornbills got their name from the large, bony bump on top of their huge beaks. Sometimes the bump is bigger than the beak itself. The bump helps to make their calls louder so they can be heard clearly through the dense jungle.

More about rainforest birds

Which is the rarest rainforest bird?

The beautiful hyacinth macaw of South America is one of the rarest birds in the rainforest. The macaw is now faced with extinction, as its forest home is being destroyed and poachers are trapping the macaw for pet dealers. As a result, there are only about 2,500 of these birds left in Brazil.

Why do antbirds follow armies of ants?

Antbirds follow armies of ants that rampage through the forests of Central and South America. Antbirds do not eat the ants, but they do eat other insects, rodents, and snakes whose habitats have been disturbed by the ants.

Which birds are the fiercest hunters?

Eagles are the fiercest hunters. Each rainforest has its own eagle: the harpy eagle in South America, the monkey-eating eagle of Asia, and the crowned eagle of Africa. Crowned eagles nest in the tallest trees on huge platforms of twigs and branches and use the same nest year after year. They are fast fliers and skilled hunters, swooping through the branches at great speeds to grab smaller birds and monkeys.

How do hanging parrots hide?

Hanging parrots in the rainforests of Asia hang upside-down from the trees. From a distance, the parrots look like bunches of leaves, so their enemies leave them alone. They also roost and even feed in this position.

How loud is a bellbird's call?

The male bellbird has one of the loudest voices of any bird. He calls to attract a female and can be heard more than half a mile away. His call sounds like a large clanging bell and if it is heard up close, the call is so piercing, it could hurt a person's ears.

Where do trogons lay their eggs?

Trogons are brightly colored birds, although the females are much duller than the males. Trogons do not build their own nests. They lay their eggs in holes they dig in abandoned ant nests in trees.

What are pittas?

Pittas are brightly colored birds from the rainforests of Asia, Australasia, and parts of Africa. They spend most of their time on the forest floor, searching for worms, insects, and snails among the leaves.

31

Which big cat rules the jungle?

The mighty jaguar, weighing up to 350 pounds, is the biggest cat in the South American rainforests. It is a solitary hunter, patrolling the forest for deer, tapirs, wild pigs, birds, and even alligators. The jaguar is an excellent climber and often drops down on its prey from the branches of a tree. It is equally at home in the water, where it hunts caimans and capybaras (the world's largest rodents). On land the jaguar's beautiful dappled coat helps the animal to hide among the forest plants, so it can surprise its prey. Sadly, so many jaguars have been hunted for their fur that they are now very rare.

More about jungle cats

Clouded leopards live in the rainforests of Southeast Asia. They spend most of their time in the trees, where they feel most at home. They hunt for birds, monkeys, squirrels, pigs, and deer. Sometimes they spring from a tree onto their unsuspecting prey.

The ocelot is a rare cat from the rainforests of Central and South America. It spends much of the day sleeping in the trees. As night falls, it hunts—not from ambush but by chasing down small mammals, birds, and snakes.

The South American margay, or tigrillo, is a small cat, about 2 feet long. It has large eyes and a long tail. The margay is one of the few animals that is at home at all 3 layers of the rainforest.

Where do orangutans live?

Orangutans live in the rainforests of Borneo and Sumatra. They are primates — a group of mammals that includes lemurs, monkeys, apes, and humans. They spend most of their time in the canopy of the rainforest, searching for the thorny fruit of the durian tree, mangoes, and figs. Orangutans also eat shoots and leaves. They have long, strong arms for swinging through the trees and are able to scoop up water and grip objects with their large hands. At night orangutans build nests out of branches and leaves for sleeping. They are an endangered species because their forest homes are being cut down for timber and to make space for farms and ranches.

More about primates

The aye-aye is a very rare and primitive lemur from Madagascar. With its bushy tail, enormous batlike ears, and huge eyes, it is one of the strangest-looking creatures in the rainforest. It uses its twiglike middle finger to poke under tree bark for juicy grubs. The aye-aye locates the grubs by listening for them in the tree bark.

If you are ever in the rainforests of Central and South America, don't be surprised if small branches start falling on top of you! Spider monkeys sometimes throw small branches at intruders to scare them away.

Every morning and evening in the Central and Southern American rainforests, groups of howler monkeys shriek and howl in chorus. They do this to warn other groups to stay away from their particular patch of forest. Howlers are the noisiest monkeys in the world and can be heard up to 5 miles away.

How slowly does a sloth move?

The three-toed sloth is found only in the rainforests of Central and South America. It gets its name because it always moves very slowly. In the trees it has a top speed of about 15 feet per minute. The sloth's long, sharp claws help the animal to firmly grip tree branches. It hangs upside-down, even when it is fast asleep. The sloth's fur often looks green because algae grow on it. This provides camouflage for the sloth in the trees and is also a source of food for caterpillars, which live in the sloth's fur.

More about rainforest animals

How do emerald tree boas climb trees?
Emerald tree boas live in the South American rainforests. They are excellent climbers, often using the hitch and hike, or concertina, method and can also wrap themselves around branches.

How does a pangolin defend itself?
The pangolin, which lives in Africa and Asia, has a covering of hard, sharp-edged scales that overlap like the tiles on a roof to provide a coat of tough, protective "armor." When danger threatens, the pangolin curls itself into a hard, tight ball to protect its soft belly.

Which are the strongest ants?
Parasol ants, also called leaf-cutting ants, are among the strongest animals on Earth for their size. A parasol ant can carry a piece of leaf that weighs 50 times more than the ant itself. This would be like a 150-pound person carrying a hippopotamus!

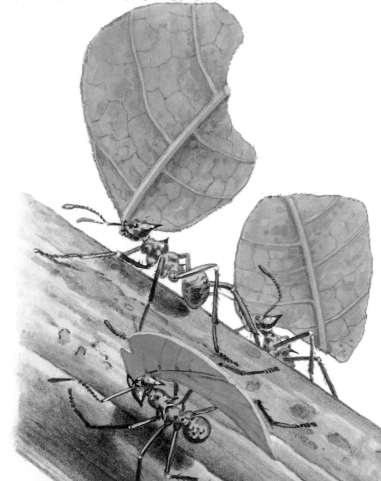

Why do chameleons change color?

Chameleons are masters of disguise. They are usually brown or green to blend with the color of the trees in which they live. However, they can change color due to changes in light and temperature or if they are angry, frightened, or sick. Some chameleons can change to black, while others can become almost white.

Which bats live in tents?

Tent-making bats from Central and South America build tentlike shelters out of large leaves. These bats are unusual because they are white. When the sunlight shines through their green tent walls, however, it makes the bats look green, too.

What sort of animal is a cuscus?

A cuscus is an odd-looking nocturnal animal with a grasping tail and staring eyes. Like the kangaroo, the cuscus is a marsupial — a mammal with a pouch on its stomach where its young develop and grow. The cuscus lives high up in the trees in Papua New Guinea, using its long tail to help it climb.

Where do royal antelopes live?

Royal antelopes live in the dense rainforests of West Africa, where they feed on leaves and fruit. They are the smallest antelopes in the world. Adults stand only 15 inches at the shoulder, and males have horns less than an inch long. They are very shy and secretive and are rarely seen.

Why do some frogs live in trees?

Many rainforest frogs live high up in the trees to avoid hungry predators on the ground. These frogs are excellent climbers. Round "suction cups" made of pads of sticky hairs on their fingers and toes help them cling to leaves, bark, or even glass. The skin on their bellies, which is loose and sticky, also helps them to grip the trees. Most tree frogs hunt for insects at night. To hide from enemies or to surprise their prey, the frogs lie on leaves that match the color of their green bodies.

More about jungle frogs

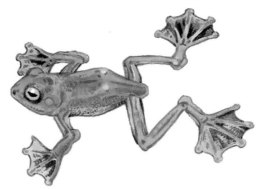

Flying frogs live in the jungles of Southeast Asia. They have large feet with long, webbed toes. When they jump from tree to tree, they spread out their webbed feet like parachutes. They can then glide down, traveling as far as 50 feet at a time.

The marine toad is found along the banks of the Amazon River. It can weigh up to 2 pounds and eats almost anything it can fit in its mouth. This includes large insects, plants, and dead animals.

The bright colors of the arrow-poison frog warn its enemies that it is very nasty to eat. Its slimy skin contains a deadly poison. One drop is strong enough to kill a large bird or monkey almost instantly. Forest hunters use the poison on the tips of their arrows and darts.

Which is the biggest rainforest spider?

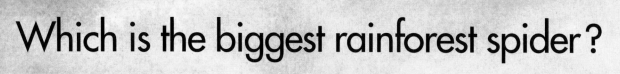

Tarantulas, sometimes called bird-eating spiders, are the biggest spiders in the world. Including their hairy legs, they can measure 10 inches across. They come out at night to hunt. They are large enough to catch tiny birds, such as hummingbirds, but this is unusual. Unlike most spiders, tarantulas do not build webs but lie in wait for their prey and then pounce. If tarantulas are attacked, they try to scare off the enemy by rising up on their back legs and baring their fangs. Despite their size, though, these spiders are normally quite peaceful and not usually harmful to humans.

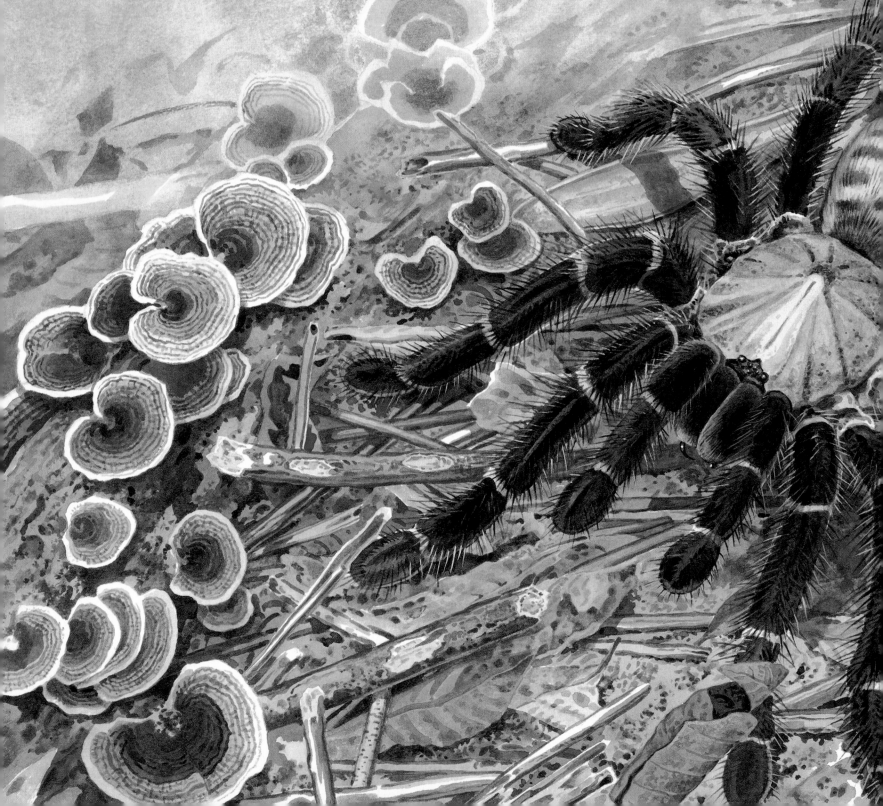

More about small creatures

Katydids are insects with superb camouflage. Some are green with veins on their wings that make them look like living leaves. Others have brown spots on their wings, so they resemble decaying leaves, and some katydids look exactly like dry, dead leaves.

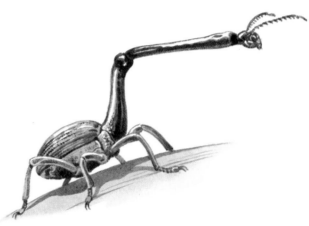

The giraffe-necked weevil of Madagascar is one of the oddest-looking rainforest insects. The male is about an inch long with a head that is about half the length of the body. No one is sure why the weevil has such an unusual head.

The orchid bee fertilizes the gongora orchid by carrying pollen from plant to plant. When an orchid bee visits a gongora orchid, the flower produces chemicals that make the bee seem drunk. It falls into the flower and gets covered with the pollen before moving on.

What color is the morpho butterfly?

A huge number of beautiful, brightly colored butterflies live in the rainforests. Some are bigger than hummingbirds. Among the most spectacular is the morpho butterfly from Central and South America. As it flits through the jungle trees, it seems to appear, then to suddenly disappear. This is because the undersides of its wings are brown for camouflage. The tops of its wings are a stunning electric-blue color. Each wingbeat produces a strobe-light effect — flashing dull brown, then electric-blue.

More about butterflies and moths

The Queen Alexandra birdwing is the biggest butterfly in the world. It lives in the rainforests of Papua New Guinea. Females have wingspans of more than 11 inches. Males are smaller. This beautiful butterfly is now very rare, due to overcollecting and the destruction of the forest.

The tent-caterpillar moth gets its name from the way its caterpillars live. They spin silk tents among the tree branches and live in them together. These moths are very good at camouflaging themselves against backgrounds such as lichen, a combination of fungi and algae, on trees.

The wild silkmoth has several ways of defending itself. It can fly away or hide among the leaves on the forest floor, where it is perfectly camouflaged. If this fails, the moth displays the huge, staring "eyes" on its wings to frighten away birds and lizards.

Index

AN ILEX BOOK
Created and produced by Ilex Publishers Limited
29-31 George Street, Oxford, OX1 2AY

Main illustrations by Robert Morton/Bernard Thornton Artists
Other illustrations by Shane Marsh/Linden Artists